Killer

Thanksgiving

Pie

A Pies and Pages Cozy Mystery

Book Four

BY

Carolyn Q. Hunter

Author's Note: On the next page, you'll find out how to access all of my books easily, as well as locate books by best-selling author, Summer Prescott. I'd love to hear your thoughts on my books, the storylines, and anything else that you'd like to comment on – reader feedback is very important to me. Please see the following page for my publisher's contact information. If you'd like to be on her list of "folks to contact" with updates, release and sales notifications, etc…just shoot her an email and let her know. Thanks for reading!

Also…

…if you're looking for more great reads, check out the Summer Prescott Publishing Book Catalog:

http://summerprescottbooks.com/book-catalog/ for some truly delicious stories.

Contact Info for Summer Prescott Publishing:

Twitter: @summerprescott1

Blog and Book Catalog: http://summerprescottbooks.com

Email: summer.prescott.cozies@gmail.com

And…look up The Summer Prescott Fan Page and Summer Prescott Publishing Page on Facebook – let's be friends! To sign up for our fun and exciting newsletter, which will give you opportunities to win prizes and swag, enter contests, and be the first to know about New Releases, click here:

https://forms.aweber.com/form/02/1682036602.htm

TABLE OF CONTENTS

PROLOGUE 10

CHAPTER 1 15

CHAPTER 2 26

CHAPTER 3 35

CHAPTER 4 45

CHAPTER 5 54

CHAPTER 6 63

CHAPTER 7 71

CHAPTER 8 86

CHAPTER 9 100

CHAPTER 10 107

CHAPTER 11 117

CHAPTER 12 126

CHAPTER 13 137

CHAPTER 14 144

CHAPTER 15 151

CHAPTER 16 159

KILLER

THANKSGIVING

PIE

A Pies and Pages Cozy Mystery
Book Four

PROLOGUE

The cough was getting worse. Tayler had been dealing with it for the last month, at least. When it had first come up, it seemed like nothing more than a normal seasonal cold. After all, since he'd been living outside on the streets, it was only natural, as the weather cooled down for the season, that he'd at least catch a bug or two.

Huddled against the brick wall in one of the alleys of the Old Market, he tried to suppress the urge to cough again. He'd spent most of his morning hidden behind the dumpster, wrapped up in his thick winter coat, and coughing like a wild man.

He had to admit, it was getting old.

In addition to the irritation of having the constant tickle in his chest, the pure fact that it was painful every time he coughed was enough to drive a man mad.

Of course, the chilly wind and the humid air weren't helping any.

Another wave rose up in his chest and he let out a series of hacks that would make a witch jealous. He gripped his chest with one hand and covered his mouth with his palm. The coughing fit seemed to last for a good thirty seconds before subsiding. "Geez," he groaned, leaning back against the wall and slumping further into the pile of autumn leaves which crunched under his weight.

If he couldn't stop this coughing soon, one of the shop owners would realize he was back there and have the cops remove him. Finding a place to rest or sleep had grown more and more difficult the stronger the cough became.

It was hard to be a silent mouse just living his existence away in the shadows when he had a built-in alarm system he couldn't turn off.

The last thing he wanted to do was move. The little pie shop where he had taken up residence the evening before gave off a lot of warmth and good smells during the daylight hours. He eagerly awaited their opening that day so he could smell the pumpkin and pecan pies which were their specialty during the Thanksgiving season. The mixture of brown sugars, roasted nuts, and flaky pie crust created a scent that made him remember better days.

It almost made him believe for a few seconds that he wasn't homeless. The holidays always seemed the worst time to be in such a dire situation.

Another attack rose up in his chest and he doubled over in pain, his lungs expanding and contracting like a recurring fiery explosion inside his body. His vision began to cross, blurring the alleyway around him. A light-headed deliriousness overtook him as his chest throbbed with pain.

For a second, he thought of an old sci-fi movie he remembered seeing in the theaters years and years ago where some strange alien creature erupted from its victim's chest.

He figured that maybe this cough was a similar feeling to that.

Lifting his palm away from his mouth, his eyes squinted up in concern.

There was bright red blood there on his glove.

Maybe, this was worse than he'd first assumed. He knew he should get up, should try and walk toward the hospital. Someone there, one of the nurses perhaps, might be willing to help him.

However, he was far too tired. He decided he would head that direction after he shut his eyes and got a little more rest, even if just for a few minutes.

Letting his eyelids flutter closed, he drifted off into a deep slumber.

CHAPTER 1

"The homeless in this city are becoming more of a problem each day, and we need to do something about it," the garbled, angry voice blared from the old-time cathedral radio in the Pies and Pages kitchen. "I suggest we instate a new law that makes loitering illegal in any part of our fine American city. I say, any homeless person found here among our streets should be picked up by local police and relocated to another place. Let's show the public a clean and safe city."

Bertha Hannah reached over and switched the station to something jazzy, silencing the woman's voice. "I'm sorry about that. I didn't know they were going to replay that this morning. Usually it's just talk radio on this station."

"That's okay," Andie Right said with a slight shrug and a sigh, "I've gotten used to her by now."

"Some mayor, huh? What kind of woman thinks it's okay to treat the homeless that way?"

Andie shook her head. "I don't even want to think about her right now. If she had her way, I'd be out of a job."

"Speaking of, I'd love to work at the soup kitchen again this year, Andie," Bertha Hannah said as she went about her usual work of rolling out the dough for the morning's pies. She'd let the crusts chill overnight in the refrigerator which made them perfect for forming into the handmade and delicate pastries she was quickly becoming famous for. "I mean, that is what you came by to ask me, right?" she smirked, knowing her old friend all too well.

"You mean it, Bert?" Andie asked, smiling as she clasped her hands, forgetting about the mayor. She was a woman about the same age as the pie shop owner. She had a gray poof of hair atop her head, the handiwork of the same salon every week for the past ten years.

Her charming cream blouse and black skirt were her usual uniform when she was heading into work for the day.

"Andie, you know more than anyone that you can count me in. Ever since Howie passed, it's been my personal tradition. After all, it's not like I have any children or other living relatives to speak of. You and Carla are my family now."

"Oh, hon, I know that," she said, reaching out in an action of comfort.

"So, yes, I'll be there Thanksgiving Day to help prepare a delicious meal for all of those in need." She placed an empty pie tin over the rolled-out crust. Flipping the whole thing, the dough rested gently into the pan.

"Great. I'm really sorry to have bothered you like this, but ever since I'd heard you'd opened this adorable little shop, I just wasn't sure you'd have the time this year."

"I'll always make time for charity," Bert beamed, trimming off the edges of the crust, so it perfectly fit the shape of the pan.

"Fantastic. I've been so shorthanded this season, and the budget's been so tight this year since our aid was cut in half, I was worried we'd not be able to have our annual Thanksgiving dinner."

Bert looked up, with her mouth slightly open in shock. "They cut your funding? I didn't know that."

Andie's mouth grew thin with worry. "Unfortunately, yes. The mayor saw to that. Things have been difficult, to say the least, and any donations have been pretty slim. I guess most people are putting their resources elsewhere. Our canned food drive made only a quarter of what we usually do."

"That's terrible."

She shrugged. "That's just the way of things sometimes. It's my job to roll with the punches, you know."

"Will you have enough for the dinner?" Grabbing the butter brush, she put a very light coat over the pie crust.

"By scrimping and saving, I think so." Sighing, she shook her head and gave a mournful smile. "I just couldn't stand to let all these men, women, and children go without something this Thanksgiving."

Bert grabbed a pinch of brown sugar and sprinkled it along the crust, making it sparkle. "I think I have an idea how I can help."

"Oh?"

"How about I make all of the pies for this year's event?"

Andie audibly gasped. "Bert, oh heavens, you can't be serious?"

She nodded. "I'm dead serious, Andie. It would be my absolute pleasure to do it."

"Oh, thank you, dear."

"What kind of pies do you think everyone would enjoy?"

"We can just stick with the staples. Pumpkin, pecan, and apple should do it."

"Great. I'll just make a note to pick up extra of everything during my shopping run tonight. That way I'll be prepared to bake up a storm tomorrow and be ready for the Thanksgiving dinner on Thursday."

"I really appreciate this."

Bert shrugged. "Aw, what are old friends for?"

Andie looked at her skinny gold watch. "Looks like I better get a move on or I'll be late. I still have a lot of preparations to make in the next two days."

"I understand."

"Thanks for letting me drop by and talk to you before business hours."

Bert let out a laugh. "Andie, it's six in the morning. Most people are still in bed while we're up and working already."

"Can't waste a single moment of life," she smiled, heading for the door and adjusting her purse over her shoulder. "I'll expect you and your pies on Thursday morning."

"I'll be there."

With one final wave of her fingers, Andie headed out into the chilly November morning.

* * *

It was getting close to ten o'clock in the morning—opening time for the Pies and Pages combination bookstore and pie shop—when Bert finished taking the last pie out of the oven. Arranging them neatly in the glass display case, she felt prepared for the bombardment of customers for the day.

Since she opened the shop in October, every week had been busier and busier, and she expected it to continue along that way until well after the new year.

Her best friend, Carla, owned a Christmas themed shop just around the corner. She had informed Bert that the Old Market district became a madhouse around the holidays.

She had been right.

Every day, the shop was full of more and more customers looking to pre-order a pie for Thanksgiving, to buy books as Christmas presents, or even just to grab a treat in between all the chaotic shopping.

Bert had plans for the month of December, including all sorts of special sales and promotions to entice new customers to stop by, but was completely swamped already with a long task list of things to do. In one respect, Andie had been right. Bert was far busier this year than previous ones.

However, Bert was determined to make time to volunteer and give back to the community, even if it seemed like a crazy idea.

She began making mental notes about how she would fit the process of baking pies for the soup kitchen in between running her own business. She figured her best option was to cook them during business hours, doing them little by little in between helping customers.

She was crossing her fingers that things would work out. It was already Tuesday, which gave her the rest of the day and the next to finish up the pies in time.

Sighing, she realized she really needed to find some other people to help out in the shop. Having even just one more employee would lighten her load considerably.

Checking her watch, she realized she had just enough time to take out the trash before she officially opened. There were many scraps and bits of rubbish from the morning's duties that had already completely filled one bag.

Tying the red pull string, she hoisted the bag from the garbage and hefted it through the storage room, through the back door, and into the alley. Setting the bag down on the pavement, she fumbled with her keys to open the lock on the dumpster.

If she didn't have the lock on there, random people tossed stuff in and cluttered it up.

Finally finding the necessary key, she undid the padlock, pulled down the safety bar, and lifted the lid. With one swoop of her arm, she tossed the bag inside and shut the dumpster closed.

Taking a deep breath and pausing for a moment to rest her hands on her knees, something strange caught her eye. A man's boot appeared to be sitting off to the side of the trash.

Perhaps someone had tried to throw it away but then realized they couldn't get the dumpster open and instead dropped it.

"People can be so inconsiderate," she whispered, reaching down and grabbing the boot. She immediately gasped and jumped back. The boot wasn't empty.

Blinking a few times to clear her sense of surprise, she got up her gumption and peeked around the dumpster. Sitting there against the brick wall of the building was a man. He had frighteningly pale skin and a hint of blood on his lips.

He appeared to be dead.

CAROLYN Q. HUNTER

CHAPTER 2

"Detective Mannor. Thank goodness you could come," Bert expelled as she saw the gruff man walk in the door. He had his usual gray trench coat on with the collar flipped up to protect against the cold. Additionally, in the last month since Bert had seen him, he'd grown out his beard a little more—not too long of course. It was professionally trimmed and well maintained. Still, it made him look like a cross between a biker and Santa. His white shirt and red tie, however, offset the whole thing with a sort of old-timey P.I. feel.

"Mrs. Hannah, good to see you again," he grunted in a none too convincing tone.

"There is a dead man in the alleyway, Detective. I'll show you the way." Bert waved, heading toward the back storeroom.

Mannor immediately held up a hand for her to stop. "No need. I've already checked it out and the coroner is taking him back to the morgue as we speak."

Bert tilted her head. "So, do you know who it is?"

"Hardly."

"And you're not going to do any investigating? Cordon off the crime scene?"

He brushed his mustache back and forth and shook his head. "No."

"No? Why not?" she protested. Since she herself had been involved in a number of homicide investigations, she was becoming more aware of the police procedures behind them.

"You have to understand. This time of year, we always get a few bums who up and croak in alleys, under bridges, you get the picture."

Bert realized her mouth was hanging open. She was a little offended by the detective's dismissive manner toward the deaths. These were humans too, men and women who ended up in a sad situation. "Doesn't he deserve a good investigation, too?"

"I only showed up because you requested me, Mrs. Hannah. This doesn't seem to be a homicide case. If anything, the guy died of a bad heart, maybe pneumonia."

"Are you serious?"

He raised one hand to silence her. "Don't worry. I have taken the liberty to sweep the alley myself, but didn't find anything significant that points to foul play."

Bert folded her arms. "So, that's it then? It wasn't a homicide and you're off the case?"

Sighing and shaking his head, he looked her in the eye. "Look, if it makes you feel better, I'll inquire about his identity myself. In the meantime, the coroner will do a full autopsy to find out an exact cause of death. If there is anything fishy going on, he'll find it."

Bert, who wasn't totally satisfied, twisted up her mouth as she looked at the Detective. However, it seemed she didn't have much of a choice in the matter, as usual.

"Look, Mrs. Hannah, not every death needs to be a murder, okay?" He clasped his hands together and pointed at her as he talked. Somehow, it felt condescending. "I appreciate all of the aid you provided in previous cases, but that won't be necessary here. It's a simple procedure of locating his family—if any—and notifying them that he has passed away."

"And if the autopsy reveals it was murder?" she pressed, realizing she was sounding crazy at this point.

Mannor raised an eyebrow. "In that case, I'll be doing a little more investigating, won't I?" He folded his arms and leaned down for a good look into her face. "But, it still won't be anything for you to worry about, now will it?"

Bert tightened her lips, a glare coming over her face.

"In either case, it's a matter for the police. Why don't you concentrate on making those delicious pies of yours?" he asked with a smirk.

"Fine," she agreed, heading back behind the counter.

"Anyway, speaking of pie, do you mind if I have a slice?" He took a leisurely seat at one of the tables. Bert wasn't sure she'd ever seen him relax. Usually, he was running about ordering officers, interrogating witnesses, or even arresting suspects.

Bert figured she probably was acting a little bit over the top in this situation. The detective was right. There was no real sign of foul play involved in this poor man's death. Bert just hated to see any person get overlooked just because they were homeless.

Realizing she needed to let the whole thing go, she put a smile back on her face. "What kind of pie would you like?"

"How about pecan?"

Bert was already in the process of getting the slice out of the dish, having thought ahead. "Got it." She lifted the plate with a smirk and waltzed over to set it in front of the detective. The slice was perfectly caramelized on top, creating a crispy brown shell along the filling. The nuts had crisped up in the baking process as well and gave off an aromatic steam.

"Thanks a million."

"I assume you're wanting a coffee with that?"

"Yes, thanks," he agreed.

Bert headed behind the counter, grabbed a clean mug, and poured the steaming hot liquid. Moving back out, she gave it to him.

"Thanks. This'll really hit the spot on a cold morning like this."

"I assume you don't have any pressing cases right now?" she said, amused by his laid-back behavior.

"Well, there is something I'm working on, but we aren't sure it really is an issue or not yet." Lifting the mug, he took a big swig and made a satisfied sigh. Picking up his fork, he sliced into the corner of the pie and ate it. A little smirk raised the corner of his mouth. "My goodness, Bert. This may be the best pie I've ever had."

She rolled her eyes. "You've said that about every pie you've had here."

"I'm simply telling the truth."

Somehow, Bert got the feeling that Detective Mannor was trying too hard.

"What is in this that makes it so good?"

"Well, it's your usual pecan pie made with brown sugar, molasses, and pecans. However, I add a touch of cinnamon, nutmeg, and ginger. I find it brings out the flavor of the nuts quite nicely."

"Well, I'd say you have a winner," he replied, lifting his fork as if he were toasting her.

She'd had enough. Placing her hands on her hips, she gave a slanted look to the policeman. "Okay. You're up to something. What is it?"

"I have no idea what you mean," he shot back, sipping his coffee again. "Besides, even if I had something on my mind, it's police related, and I can't share it with you."

Bert wasn't buying it, but knew that the man was more stubborn than she was.

She wouldn't get anything out of him.

CHAPTER 3

After closing down the shop that evening, Bert decided to stop by the soup kitchen to see Andie again. She'd spent much of the day going over the schedule in her mind. She was having trouble seeing where she could possibly fit in making enough pies for the Thanksgiving dinner at the kitchen. However, on her way out she had an idea pop into her head.

Climbing into her car, she drove out of the Old Market district of town and into the main downtown hub of Culver's Hood, Nebraska. The area had a major library, the police station, the firehouse, and—of course—the soup kitchen.

Most of the homeless people of the city could be found in the downtown area begging for extra cash or a little food. The soup kitchen provided them with some place to go to rather than staying out on the streets.

It wasn't perfect, but it at least fed some people in need.

Pulling up outside the front doors, the nightly arrangement of patrons was already waiting in line for a warm bowl of soup, some freshly baked bread, and a cup of hot coffee.

Bert nodded genially at a few of the men as she walked into the building.

Stepping among the tables, she glanced behind the counter to see if Andie was there. The only person standing there was a young and pretty Hispanic woman dressed in the usual hair-net and apron. She was ladling out soup to the men and woman waiting in line.

"Hello," Bert greeted the woman as she approached the counter.

"Evening," the girl smiled in reply. There was a small twinkle in her hazelnut eyes. "Can I help you with something?"

Bert, not wanting to stand in the way of the line, took the liberty of stepping behind the serving counter. Checking the woman's volunteer nametag, she smirked. "Shiv, is it?"

"That's right, but you can't be back here in the kitchen area. It's against regulation."

"Don't worry. I'm a volunteer."

"Oh?"

"Well, Shiv, I was actually looking for Andie. I wanted to ask her about the ovens here for Thanksgiving Day."

"The ovens?" Shiv raised a confused eyebrow.

"Oh, I'm sorry. You see, I'm going to be baking the pies for Thanksgiving dinner here in the kitchen."

The girl's eyes widened with recognition. "Oh, that's right. Andie did mention that someone had volunteered to donate the pies."

"Yep, that's me. Unfortunately, I'm a little strapped for time and was hoping there would be oven space the day of. That way I could prepare the pies ahead of time and then bake them right here in the kitchen."

Turning her head slightly, Shiv eyeballed the row of three rusty old industrial ovens. "I guess you could, if you're willing to trust those junkers."

"Junkers? Do they not work anymore?"

"Oh, they work, just not well. It's like everything else here," she admitted with a solemn look in her eye.

For the first time since arriving, Bert took an honest look around the room. Beat up and dented metal counters lined the walls, chipped tile floors lay below her feet, tarnished cooking utensils hung on the walls, and there was even a small metal cage just below the stove. It was almost like standing on the set of some horror movie.

"Dare I ask what that cage is for?"

Shiv sighed, dropping her voice to a low whisper so that the patrons couldn't hear. "A catch and release rat trap."

"There are seriously rats here?" Bert asked, whispering

"Sometimes they get in through the vents at night. Not often, but enough that it's a concern. I've told Andie she should invest in some rat poison, but she insists on only using catch and release methods. I swear, if the health inspector finds out he won't hesitate to close us. He's always looking for a reason to shut down the soup kitchen."

"Why would he want to do that?" Bert asked.

"He's in the mayor's pocket. Like her, he thinks it encourages homeless people to hang around downtown. He cares about how the city looks, but just goes about it the wrong ways, I think."

"Wow, I'm sorry to hear all that. I mean, Andie told me things were tight, but I wasn't aware it was this bad."

"Well, that's just how things work sometimes. Less and less money is given to help those in need and more is put toward useless junk like parking meters."

"All of these setbacks must make cooking here difficult."

"Well, I wouldn't call this cooking." She stirred the grayish soup with an adamant twirl of her wrist.

"Oh?"

"Canned soups with a little added veggie? Frozen bread that we bake up in faulty ovens? Instant coffee? No, it isn't cooking. Even a little touch of spices, some thyme, a pinch of paprika, could really make this more palatable. Heck, I've even asked if I could have the ingredients to bake some fresh loaves of bread, but Andie just says there is no money for it."

Bert leaned on the counter. "That really is sad. I bet you would make a good cook if given a chance."

"I'd love to do some real cooking, work in a real kitchen. However, this place helped me eat many times when I was growing up, so it only seems fitting to give back."

"Goodness," Bert mumbled, her face growing warm and red. It always hurt Bert's heart to see the kind of people who were forced to turn to community services. Shiv seemed like such a sweet girl, and she hated to think of her living on the streets.

"You're surprised to hear that I used to eat here?"

"No, no, not at all. I'm glad you had someplace to go. I just feel a little embarrassed for going on and on about pies and giving back to the community, about helping these people, when you yourself used to be in the same situation not that long ago."

"Don't worry about it, okay? I'm happy to be here to help." She slopped some more soup into a bowl and handed it over the counter. "At least it gives me something to do while I figure things out, look for a job."

Bert blinked slowly as an idea popped into her head.

"What? You're surprised I don't have a job, too? Let me guess, you think I'm entitled and lazy?"

"Oh, my goodness, no. Not at all. I was actually thinking that, if you're okay with it, you could come and work for me at my shop."

"Oh, yeah? Doing what?" Shiv replied in a somewhat interested tone.

"Actually, I run a pie shop."

Shiv looked up from her work over the pot of soup and directly at Bert. "Y-you mean that Pies and Pages place?"

"Why, yes. So, you've heard of it?"

"Heard of it? Only every food blogger is talking about you." she shrugged, a hint of embarrassment in her cheeks. "I mean, I usually like to go to the library and read about the latest food trends. Food has always been sort of a passion for me, I guess. In some ways, spicing things up helped me get through some tough moments in my life."

Bert held out a hand. "Well, I'm pleased to meet a fellow foodie. My name is Bertha Hannah, but you can call me Bert."

"Wait, you're serious about a job?"

"Darn right."

"You don't even know me."

"I know enough about you to know that you're a girl with character. You work hard, and you have passion. I think you'll make a great addition to my shop."

Shiv half smirked and tilted her head. "How do you know I won't just rob you or something?"

Bert placed a hand on the girl's forearm. "Trust me. I'm a great judge of character."

"Bert, oh my, I didn't know you were here," a familiar voice echoed from the back room.

"Andie, just the woman I was looking for." Bert looked at Shiv one more time and patted her arm. "We'll talk later, I promise." After that, she headed back into Andie's office.

CHAPTER 4

L uckily for Bert, everything looked like it was going to work out. Even if the ovens were a little faulty, she was willing to take the chance on them if it meant she could relax a little more on her pie making duties. Better than that, she had a new employee coming in to help in the shop once the Thanksgiving weekend had ended. (She was refusing to do any sort of Black Friday sales and instead was closing down until Monday in protest of the "tradition.")

After her visit to the soup kitchen, Bert made a quick visit to the nearest big box store—the kind that sold everything in bulk sizes—and picked up everything she would need including three sugar pumpkins, two bags of brown sugar, two large packages of raw pecans, and extra cinnamon, cardamom, and nutmeg for good measure.

The next morning, she got up extra early—around three a.m.—to go to the shop and get to work on the pies. Despite the hour, she felt invigorated with the spirit of the holiday. The idea that she would be giving to people in need, people who might be able to come out of it like Shiv, seemed like a real blessing.

(Of course, the cup of pumpkin spiced double-shot coffee from The Koffee Hous was helping to boost her spirits as well.)

By opening time at ten o'clock, she'd already finished all the pies for the Thanksgiving event, which were ready to bake as soon as she arrived at the soup kitchen the next day, as well as the ones she would sell in the shop during the day. Now, all that needed to be done, was prepare the orders that customers were going to pick up for their own Thanksgiving dinners.

"Good morning," Carla called as she stepped in the front door.

"Hey, Carla. I thought you'd be over at your own shop this morning," Bert commented upon seeing her best friend waltzing between the tables and leaning on the counter.

"Oh, I have Jordon watching it."

"I think you maybe take advantage of that girl, you know?" she pointed out.

Carla waved a dismissive hand. "Never mind that. Look at this morning's paper."

Bert put her nose in the air in a fake show of pride. "I already did. The comics and arts sections because that's all that's worth looking at."

Carla lifted her own copy of the paper and slapped it on the glass counter. "You didn't see this?" she insisted, pointing at the opened page.

Glancing down, the pie shop owner shrugged. "A local camera shop was robbed three times this week?"

Rolling her eyes, her friend laid her finger on the page. "No. This," she exclaimed.

Bert's eyes wandered over and read the title of the article. *Rise in Homeless Deaths. Police Suspect Poisoning.* She immediately gasped, grabbing up the paper from her friend.

"I know you said you found that guy behind your shop yesterday when we had lunch together. I just never realized he could be poisoned."

"I knew he was hiding something," Bert snipped.

"Who? Detective Mannor?" Carla asked, twiddling her thumbs as she eyed the variety of pies in the case.

Bert twisted her lips to the side. "Who else? He was acting so strange yesterday, like he didn't want me to figure something out."

"That the guy behind your shop was murdered?"

Bert nodded. "I specifically asked him about it. I mean, he is a homicide detective. Why else would he show up on the scene?" She shook her head.

"Maybe because you asked for him?" she suggested, wiggling her eyebrows.

Bert tilted her head at her friend. "No. He was here because he's on the case of these strange deaths of homeless people. Now I find out that they're being poisoned." She flipped the paper up in front of her and read the details of the story.

"Doesn't that seem a little weird? I mean, the reporters are saying it could be like a serial killer or something."

Scanning the words, Bert gave a knowing nod. "Either they are all being poisoned on accident, by the same source, or someone is targeting them."

"With rat poison? I think it's on purpose. We have a psycho running around the streets killing people," Carla squeaked nervously.

"Is that what it is?" Bert asked, looking more closely at the article.

"Anticoagulant rodenticide is what it says. That's rat poison, you know."

"How do you know that?"

She shrugged. "About a year back we had a few in the shop, so I bought the stuff. These are old buildings, you know."

Bert nodded.

"I'd heard that it's real dangerous, though, because rats have adapted to the poisons over the years. The companies have had to increase the potency, making it harmful or even deadly to humans. I made sure to do all my research before using the stuff. I didn't want to accidentally poison myself or one of the customers."

Bert half smirked. "I don't think you can poison yourself unless you eat it."

"You never know," she replied with a serious, furrowed brow.

Bert tried not to laugh at her friend.

Carla didn't notice the humored smirk on her friend's lips. She was too deep in thought, tapping her fingers on the counter. "Maybe the food at the soup kitchen you always volunteer at is contaminated for some reason."

"Well, that place isn't exactly up to code, but I doubt rat poison would find its way into the soup. Besides, they don't even have it on the premises. Andie and one of her volunteers told me so last night. They use strictly catch and release tactics."

Carla shook her head. "You couldn't catch me doing that. I want them dead and gone for good."

"Yeah, but some people think it's more humane to catch them, and I tend to agree."

Carla waved her hand again. "Whatever suits you."

"In any case, unless the pots and pans there are contaminated with rat poison—which I highly doubt—I'd say we're dealing with a killer here. Someone is targeting the homeless and somehow feeding it to them." Bert groaned, leaning in on the counter herself.

"This time of year, it could be almost anyone. All sorts of charities, businesses, and organizations are handing things out. Charitable food pantries, day old breads from the bakery around the corner, even the thrift store gives out free coffee to the homeless."

"What are you going to do about it?" Carla pressed.

Bert looked up at her friend and shook her head. "Absolutely nothing. Detective Mannor is right. This is a police matter, and they can handle it on their own. They don't need an old busybody like me poking around into their business."

"I suppose."

Bert stood up from the counter. "In any case, I'm way too busy this week to be worrying about murder. I've got more pies to make."

Carla smiled. "Speaking of pies, do you think I could get a slice of pecan before I head back?"

CHAPTER 5

"Bert, good morning," Andie beamed as she answered the knock at the kitchen's back door. The owner of Pies and Pages stood there with her arms filled with a tall stack of Tupperware containers with the pre-prepared pies inside.

"Morning, coming through," she sounded off, pushing into the kitchen and frantically looking for a place to set the containers. She'd clearly tried to carry too many in a single trip and was faltering under the encumbrance.

"Happy Thanksgiving," Andie chimed, not realizing how much her friend was struggling.

"Where can I set these?" she pleaded.

"Oh, dear, I'm sorry. Right there on the counter." Andie motioned to the clear space on the pockmarked metal surface.

Almost hobbling at that point, Bert waddled over and slid the pies off. Making sure they were settled safely, she let out a sigh of relief.

"Sheesh, you'd think I could be a better help rather than just standing here like a goon wishing you a happy Thanksgiving," Andie fretted, scolding herself.

Bert smiled widely and looked at her friend. "And a happy Thanksgiving to you as well."

"You always were very forgiving."

Bert laughed delightedly. To her, the heavy load of the pies was a minor thing. It was one of her absolute favorite holidays, and one tiny mishap wasn't going to ruin that. "I'm not the kind of person to hold a grudge, it's true. Especially over something as silly as you not helping me carry the pies."

"Still. You were always the most charitable and helpful person in the congregation," she admitted. At one point a few years back, the two ladies had attended the same church. It was actually how Bert had learned about the soup kitchen and began volunteering. The congregation sometimes even all volunteered together, but not as often recently.

"Speaking of church, why don't I see you there anymore on Sundays?"

Shutting the door to keep out the cold blustering winds, Andie gave a little shrug. "I'm pretty busy these days."

Bert nodded. "Believe me, I understand."

"I know it's where a lot of people go for help—emotionally, spiritually, that sort of thing. But, I had a hard time seeing all of those friends who were suffering or going through hard times. I just can't stand to see anyone suffer and not be able to do anything about it."

"Well, you do work at a soup kitchen, you know?" Bert stepped back up to the doorway.

"I know, but at least I'm doing something useful here."

"Is that why you catch rats and release them back into the wild?" she teased, not wanting to make her friend feel uncomfortable in any way, especially on Thanksgiving.

Andie's smile returned. "I know they can have a happy existence outside, so I give it to them. If I thought I couldn't help them, I'd just use poison like everyone else, I guess."

"It also helps to know that they're not in your walls anymore," Bert laughed out loud.

"Definitely," she said, her smile widening. "What can I help you with?"

"I still have a few more stacks of pies outside in the car, if you don't mind helping."

"I'd love to. Shiv can help us, too."

Bert glanced around with a curious eye. "Shiv is here too? I didn't see her."

"She's out front decorating the dining room. We want everything to feel festive for the men, women, and families who come in here today. Of course, I had to buy all the decorations with my own money. There was no way I could use our measly budget on it. We can barely afford any sort of worthwhile food to give them."

"I'm sure it will be lovely," Bert agreed, walking toward the dining room.

"I'm telling you, Bert. Those pies are really going to make a big difference in today's meal," Andie added as she followed her friend.

"I'm just glad to help in any way I can," she admitted. Passing the serving counter, she spotted the young woman standing on a step ladder in the corner. She was hanging a red, orange, and brown garland that was embellished with happy looking cartoon turkeys.

"Morning, Shiv," Bert called to her.

Turning around, the young woman beamed. There was just something about Thanksgiving that brought out the glow in people. Bert hoped to see that look on many faces that day.

"Bert, you're here early."

"I said I was going to bake the pies in the ovens here, and that's what I intend to do."

"Maybe you can help decorate a little too," she added.

"I think that sounds great, but first, do you mind helping Andie and I bring the pies in from the car?"

Pinning up the end of the garland, Shiv climbed down. "I'm all hands. Besides, I better get used to handling pies if I'm going to be working for you," she joked.

"Oh, you didn't tell me this, Bert. Are you stealing away one of my best volunteers?" Andie chimed in, clearly thrilled to have Shiv finally getting a job.

"Yes, ma'am. I'm sorry to do it to you," Bert answered.

"Hey, I love to volunteer, but I've gotta pay bills, too," Shiv added.

"Believe me, I'm happy for you, dear. It's about time you found some work, and you couldn't pick a better employer."

Bert shook her head and rolled her eyes at her friend's flattery. "Shall we grab those pies?"

"Let's," Andie agreed.

Bert took the lead, heading past the counter and into the kitchen. Opening the back door, she allowed the two ladies through and then walked out herself. "There are just a few more stacks," she said, digging into her pocket for her keys. For a moment, they got stuck on something and Bert was forced to give them a good yank.

Coming free from her pocket, a few quarters and a couple dollar bills went wild. The change rolled along the ground, and the bills floated in the chilly November breeze. "Oh, darn," she grumbled. She hit the button to unlock the car. It beeped indicating it was open. "Go ahead and start grabbing the pies while I pick up this money."

"Got it," Shiv noted.

Bert grabbed most of the bills, and even the quarters, before they got too far. However, one bill had continued its path across the alleyway, forcing Bert to make chase. Another gust came up, tossing the bill about with a handful of autumn leaves. "Oh, poo," she complained, watching it float up above her head and then come back down.

As she watched it land among a pile of garbage bags, she stopped cold. For a second, she didn't believe her eyes, and thought it had to be a trick of the light against the sacks. However, she quickly realized it was no trick.

There, among the bags, was another man in tattered clothing—clearly homeless. The front of his shirt was tainted with blood and holes revealed stab wounds underneath.

He clutched a crushed micro-camera in his right hand.

"Oh, dear," she muttered.

CHAPTER 6

"So, what do you think this time, Detective? Is this just another random homeless death?" Bert spoke in an accusatory and scathing tone upon seeing the trench coat wearing man enter the dining area through the kitchen. She didn't mean to be so harsh, or so forward, but something about finding two dead men in back alleyways in as little as two days had that strange effect on her.

As soon as the remark had slipped out between her lips, she wished she could slurp it back in.

As the lines in Detective Mannor's face deepened from serious to angry, Bert could feel her own cheeks growing red hot with embarrassment. She felt for sure that he would slap her with some sort of minor violation this time. She'd had her fair share of tense encounters with the detective, and had stood to be fined on multiple other occasions where she'd found herself in the middle of an investigation.

"Officer, she didn't mean that. She's just a little shaken up after finding that poor man in the alleyway, is all," Andie jumped in, hoping to defuse the situation.

The pinched look at the corners of his eyes didn't subside, but it was clear he was biting his tongue. "Mrs. Hannah, if you'd prefer to handle this investigation on your own," he said in an even voice through a heavy sigh.

She put up both hands and waved them defensively. "No, no, my apologies. Andie is right. I'm just a little overwhelmed is all. You're the professional here." She diverted to his judgment, hoping her brief lapse of tongue wouldn't cost her too dearly.

"Good. I'm glad you see it that way."

Andie stood up from the table with her cup of coffee in hand, the steam rising to greet her face. "So, Detective, is it true? Was that poor man really murdered?"

Looking down at his feet, his hands firmly on his hips, he let out a low grunt. "I'm afraid so."

Slowly sinking back into her chair, not unlike a balloon that had sprung a small leak, Andie turned deathly pale. "Oh, dear. I had hoped it was all a mistake."

"There isn't much to mistake here, Mrs.?"

"Andie Right."

"Mrs. Right. This man was clearly stabbed to death. I can guarantee it was murder."

"Do you think his death has anything to do with all of the recent poisonings of local homeless people?" Bert asked before she could stop the curiosity from slipping out.

Mannor shot a glare her direction, his eyes nearly disappearing behind strained eyelids.

Why couldn't she just keep her darn mouth shut?

"Where did you hear that?" he asked through his teeth, his breath whistling slightly with each word.

Why did she have the feeling that this wasn't supposed to be public knowledge?

"Sorry, it was in the newspaper yesterday morning," she admitted.

"Dang those reporters," he snapped, more to himself than anyone else.

"Wait, wait. Are you saying that there has been a series of these homeless murders?" Andie exclaimed, sitting up straight in her chair.

"I can't comment on an ongoing investigation," he sniffed, not liking how this conversation was going. Clearly, he had come in intending to be the one asking the questions. In his usual manner, he'd interrogate the ladies, get the information he wanted, and send them on their way. It was the same series of events that always played out, at least in Bert's experience with the man.

He was older, stuck in his ways, and had a very specific method for going about a homicide investigation.

However, ever since Bert had shown up, it had thrown a wrench in his works.

She could tell he was getting tired of it.

"But it's true, isn't it?" Bert butted in, unable to help herself. She was a woman who liked organization and safety. If she had the ability, she always was looking to help. Sometimes, that made her seem like a busybody.

"Excuse me?"

"It was in the paper, which means somebody told the reporters about your ongoing investigation." She left out the part where she had suspected the detective was up to something even before the story was released.

Mannor set his jaw, the muscles tensing uncomfortably. "Someone obviously blabbed," he muttered.

"So, it might be connected," she affirmed.

"Mrs. Hannah," he sneered quietly.

"And what about that broken camera he was holding?" She continued on, asking questions. Her confidence, and her need to figure things out, had kicked into high gear and overtaken her worry about the detective's reaction.

"That was a camera? But it was so small," Andie exclaimed.

"Enough. No more questions," Detective Mannor barked.

The women fell into silence, staring down into their respective cups of coffee. Shiv, on the other hand, looked hardly phased at all.

"If anyone is going to be asking any questions, it's me. Do we understand each other?" he demanded, passing his eyes from one woman to the next.

Clearly, this whole series of murders had been a lot to handle already for the detective. He was at his wit's end, and the last thing he needed was a couple of nosy women making unnecessary inquiries into his work.

"Do we understand?" he reiterated.

Both women nodded.

"Okay, then. Let's get on with this."

CHAPTER 7

Bert clenched her jaw, trying not to reply with another foolish insult like before. She didn't like being yelled at or put down—and she rarely stood for that sort of treatment. In this case, however, she was quiet. After all, she had stepped outside her bounds by asking so many prying questions into the detective's homicide case.

Clearly, he had tried to keep this information from her the other day because he was afraid of something exactly like this happening.

Bert couldn't help herself sometimes. Not to mention, her friend Andie was very upset by this whole ordeal, and Bert wanted to help her feel as comfortable as possible. The idea that someone was stabbed to death right behind your place of work wasn't exactly the coziest thing in the world.

"Now, then," the detective cleared his throat, looking over the trio of women sitting at the table sipping coffee. When he'd arrived with his team of officers, he had instructed them to sit in the dining area and not move from it. The room was half-decorated with the colors of autumn. Streamers went partway around the walls, but then hung sadly to the floor partway through. A pile of other paper and cardboard items sat in a pile at the end of one of the long tables. These were all whispers and hints of the upcoming Thanksgiving dinner that same evening. Bert wondered if the detective was going to shut them down and cancel the whole event.

If he did that, she wasn't sure she could restrain her tongue.

Mannor's eyes fell on Shiv like he was seeing her for the first time, his head tilting in curiosity. His face visibly softened to a point that he almost looked like he could be someone's grandpa. "I apologize for my outburst, young lady."

His sudden change of attitude, and the chime in his voice, was shocking. Bert looked from the detective, to Shiv, and back at the detective again. What did this mean?

He was being civil, even kind, to the young woman.

"That's alright. I understand," Shiv finally answered with a little unsure nod.

Pulling his usual handy-dandy notepad from his pocket, the detective flipped the pages back open. The little leather pad looked worn to death, like it had lived the last ten years in that pocket. It was the kind that had refillable pages, but it looked like it was time to replace the pad itself as well. "Do you mind telling me your name?"

The young woman sat up straight as she answered him in a proper and respectful voice. "Shiv Hart."

He poised his pen, ready to write it down, but paused. "Do you mind spelling that for me?"

"First name, S-H-I-V. Last name, H-A-R-T."

Mannor scribbled the name down. "Okay. Thank you."

Bert strained to think of any other time she remembered the detective saying thank you for something and actually meaning it. She came up blank.

"And you said your name is Andie Right?"

"Correct, and it's spelled A-N-D-I-E."

"And the last name's with a W?"

"No, without."

He wrote it down. "And what is your business here at the soup kitchen today?"

Andie's mouth quivered slightly, her jaw moving up and down, as she tried to formulate words. "I-I'm the director here."

"I see."

"Detective, you don't think that I or either of these ladies had anything to do with this, do you?" she gasped weakly, placing one hand on Bert and Shiv's arms, respectively.

He raised an eyebrow, wondering if this woman was going to cause him any trouble like Bert always seemed to. "No, ma'am. I'm just asking some preliminary questions at the moment."

"Oh, I see."

"And you, ma'am?" he asked, looking at Shiv.

"M-Me? What about me?"

"Do you work here as well?"

"She's one of my volunteers," Andie chimed in.

Mannor looked at the director with a squint of his eye. "I was asking the young lady."

"Sorry."

"She's correct. I am a volunteer here," Shiv confirmed the information.

"And one of my absolute best," Andie replied, patting the girl's hand.

"I've been coming here every day for the past year, helping out while I look for work."

Mannor smiled. "That's very admirable." His eyes, suddenly growing slim with irritation again, turned on Bert. "And what are you doing here this time?"

Bert bit her lower lip to keep from blurting out a rude remark. She folded her arms and leaned back in her chair, taking a deep breath. "I'm a volunteer as well. I'm making all the pies for this year's dinner."

"Dinner?" He tapped his pen on the pad.

Andie jumped in to answer this time. "That's right. It's Thanksgiving Day after all. We always have a special dinner for anyone in need. It's an annual tradition, you see."

Mannor gave a brief nod and a grunt in reply. "I see." He was staring down at his notepad, screwing up his face with thought.

Bert didn't like that look. It seemed to her that maybe he was planning on shutting them down temporarily.

"Now, you were here earliest this morning?" he looked at Andie.

"Yes. I wanted to be here bright and early to help get things set up for this evening."

"I see. And what time was that?"

"Just around six."

"And which way did you come in?" He motioned with his pen from the front door to the back.

"The back door, from the alley. I always come in that way."

After scribbling this down, Mannor looked her closely in the eye. "And was there a body out there then?"

"Of course, not. Not that I saw anyway."

"Detective, it appeared the body was shoved behind the dumpster. She could have easily missed it. I know I did at first," Bert commented.

"No, no. I came up the alley from the other side," Andie admitted, pointing the opposite direction.

"From State Street?"

She nodded. "The parking meters are cheaper over there, so I always considered it worth it just to walk a few extra feet."

"So, you're saying you might have seen the body?"

She tapped the side of her mug with a pink manicured nail. "That is precisely what I'm saying. I would have seen him. He simply wasn't there yet."

Mannor hummed thoughtfully before turning to look at Shiv again. "And what time did you get here, Ms. Hart?"

"Just before six-thirty."

"And which way did you come up the alley?"

"Well, I don't have a car. I took the bus and got off at the stop on State Street."

"So, you didn't see a body either?"

She shook her head. "It wasn't there. I swear it."

"Don't worry. I believe you," he said comfortingly.

Bert tried not to sneer at his strange sense of sincerity. What was this? Did he just treat young and pretty women better?

"So, Mrs. Hannah, you're the only one who came up from the opposite end?"

"That's right. And that was at seven this morning, if you'd like to know." She tacked on the time assuming that was going to be his next questions.

Mannor tried to hide his distaste at this. "And you all found the body when?"

"At five or ten after seven, about," Andie added.

"Do any of you ladies know the gentlemen who was found in the alley this morning?"

Bert shook her head, "no," and looked at Andie expectantly. The detective was doing the same.

She could only shrug. "I'm sorry, Detective, I've never seen the man before."

"He'd never come into the soup kitchen for food?"

"Never."

There was an uncomfortable pause as Mannor scribbled down the notes.

"I-I've seen him," Shiv chimed in, quiet as a mouse.

Both women and the detective looked at her with wide eyes. "You know him, Shiv?" Andie exclaimed.

She nodded.

"Who is it?" Detective Mannor pressed.

"Well, you see, I don't know him, know him. I've just seen him in here once is all."

"Go on," he encouraged her.

"Well, you see, he came in a few days ago and tried to sweet talk me."

"You mean he made advances toward you?"

"Sort of. He seemed drunk. At first, he kept asking if he could see a pretty girl like me in private. He even suggested we step into the back part of the kitchen."

"And what did you say in reply to this?"

"I told him no, of course. I wasn't about to let him into the back. That's against policy."

"I see. Then what happened?"

"Well, he got sort of angry, tried to push his way back into the kitchen. I had to block the way and force him back out."

"Did he hurt you at all?"

She shook her head. "Not really. He was too drunk to really try very hard. He didn't seem to have much balance. Still, he stank and was rude." She shivered. "He sort of scared me."

"Did you have to call any sort of help to remove him?"

"No. Eventually, he gave up and left."

Mannor's smile for her had all but vanished. Bert didn't like what that might mean. "Thank you for your help, ladies. I'll request that you all head home for the day."

"Home for the day?" Andie squeaked.

"That's right. I'm going to have to close down the soup kitchen while we finish investigating."

Bert felt her heart sink as she watched her friend's face go pale.

"B-but, what about the Thanksgiving meal for the homeless? We have hundreds of people counting on us for a decent dinner this evening." Andie's eyes were beginning to turn red, a sure sign of tears.

"My apologies, Mrs. Right. That isn't my main concern at the moment."

"Don't you have a heart?" Bert exclaimed, standing up and slamming her hands on the table.

"Mrs. Hannah. The last thing I need is another accusation from you."

"These people, these families, rely on this soup kitchen. It's a holiday, and many of them have nowhere else to go."

Mannor shook his head. "I'm sorry."

"How can you do this?"

Andie stood up and touched Bert on the shoulder, basically telling her to let it go.

"Now please, all of you, head home or I'll have one of my men escort you out." With that, the detective disappeared back through the kitchen door.

As soon as he was out of sight, Andie slumped back into her own chair. "What are we going to do?"

"Maybe we could find somewhere else to do it?" Shiv added hopefully.

Andie only shook her head. "All of our food is back there. We couldn't possibly get it all again."

Suddenly, Bert had an idea. "It'll mean a lot of extra work, and there might not be the same kind of meal or space for everyone, but maybe we could move it to my shop."

"Bert? We couldn't do that."

"Of course, we can. At the very least, we can work hard to make up some pies. They can at least have a yummy slice of something warm, even if we can't give them a full meal."

Andie clasped her hands thankfully and nodded. "Okay. Let's do it."

CHAPTER 8

S ince the majority of the decorations at the soup kitchen hadn't been hung yet, and they were all in the front area where none of the cops were, the woman gathered them up and took them along. Additionally, they whipped up a few signs from extra construction paper and felt markers to help inform anyone who showed up at the soup kitchen that they could head over to Pies and Pages for a Thanksgiving treat.

Bert had to ride in the same car with Andie and Shiv. Technically, her car had ended up behind the police tape in the crime scene. She wouldn't have it back until the next day at the earliest, unless the detective found something "pertinent to the case" and decided to hold it for longer.

Needless to say, Bert wasn't thrilled about the idea. She'd just have to ask Carla for rides until this whole mess was cleared up.

Arriving at Pies and Pages, the three woman got fast to work getting the place ready. Shiv rushed to get all the decorations hung throughout the quaint pie and bookstore. The tables were draped with red and brown plastic cloths and cute fold out centerpieces in the shape of turkeys were put on each one.

At the same time, Bert got to working like a madwoman in the kitchen to prepare new pies to replace the ones left at the crime scene. Luckily, she had plenty of extra ingredients left over from her shopping trip to make a new set of delicious desserts.

Meanwhile, Andie worked to call in a few favors. She hoped to dredge up some last-minute food donations to round out the Thanksgiving meal into more than just a pie fest.

Within the hour, and much to the shock of the three hard-working women, shop owners from all over the Old Market district, as well as members from Bert's church congregation, were arriving with their arms full of food products. Boxes of stuffing, packets of gravy, cans of green beans and cranberry sauce, and even a few extra turkeys found their way into the small kitchen area.

None of it was gourmet eating, and not a lot of it would be made from scratch, but this at least meant they could have something for the homeless to eat.

Bert ran around like a crazy woman, attempting to find the best ways to utilize the dishes she had to cook everything. Having multiple ovens sure made things easier.

It was getting to be afternoon, and the whole shop was feeling festive. The decorations added a splash of seasonal color while the aroma of a true Thanksgiving meal permeated the air. "Here you go," a voice called as the door opened for probably the hundredth time that day.

"Carla! Happy Thanksgiving," Bert beamed upon seeing her friend. She wore her orange, brown, and white plaid apron which was coated in spots of flour dust and sugar.

Carla walked over to the counter and set down the hefty turkey she had cradled in her arms. "I brought over a turkey for you."

Bert eyed the giant bird before her. "Carla, it's huge! Where did you find it so last minute?"

Smiling, she waved a hand at her friend. "Oh, it was easy. I just opened my fridge and there it was."

"Oh, no, Carla. It's your own Thanksgiving turkey?"

"And now it's yours."

"No, we couldn't possibly take it."

Carla made a tisking noise in the back of her throat. "You can, and you will."

"But what will you eat?"

"Well, you see, none of my kids can make it out this year. I bought this when I thought they were going to make the trip. Turned out, none of them are going to show up. It would be a waste to just make it and eat it alone."

"You were going to be alone today? Why didn't you tell me?"

"Oh, I didn't want to worry you."

"Carla, you're like family. You can always tell me."

"Well, in any case, I figured, what better way to use it then giving it to those in need. Besides, I prefer to spend my holiday here with you, my best friend."

Bert was smiling so wide at this point that she thought her lips just might stretch off her face. Her vision blurred slightly with tears of gratitude, but she pushed them back as she grabbed her best friend and embraced her in a tight hug. "Thank you. I'm so happy you're here."

"You better get things started, then," Carla said.

"You're right. We don't have much time left, so we better get moving." Bert lifted the turkey and hoisted it into the sink. Cooking this guy up would be a close call, but she thought she could have it ready by the time the other smaller turkeys were eaten up.

"What can I do to help?"

"Do you mind chopping those pecans into smaller pieces for the pie?" she motioned to the large bag on the counter.

"On it." Carla instinctively grabbed one of the extra aprons off the hook. "Mind if I use this?"

"Be my guest."

Slipping it over her head, she tied the ends and picked up the cutting knife to get to work. "I'm so sad to hear about the murder at the soup kitchen. Even on a holiday, there seems to be horrible things happening in the world."

"That's true, but there are plenty of great things going on as well. I mean, look at how everyone in the community came together to make this happen when it seemed the police had shut it down for good."

Carla glanced around the room at all the people who had shown up to donate food or volunteer time at the last minute. "You're right. There is nothing quite like it."

"I was really upset earlier, too, but it looks like things are going to really work out well."

"So, do you think this murder is related to those other deaths we read about in the paper?" she asked, chopping the nuts vigorously.

Bert sighed, thinking of her encounter with Detective Mannor that morning. "I can almost guarantee it. I don't think the detective would have been so mad at me otherwise. I mean, for heaven sake, you'd think he blamed me for his case ending up in the papers."

"Well, somebody spilled the beans. That's for sure."

"It's true, but who? Who would possibly know that all of those people were being poisoned and murdered if they weren't part of the force?"

"Maybe the murderer tipped off the news agencies. I hear serial killers really like the attention."

Bert rolled her eyes. "I'm not so sure we can call it a serial killer yet. We don't know much about this case."

"It does seem odd that the man you found this morning was stabbed. Maybe it's a completely unrelated crime?"

"Maybe," Bert agreed. However, something in her gut was tingling, telling her otherwise. Deep down, she knew that all the deaths were connected. The stabbing made it even clearer that these were all murders, not sad accidents.

"Didn't you mention that the dead guy had a broken camera on him?" Carla asked, referring to the phone conversation they'd had just a few hours earlier. Bert had called Carla and asked her to help spread the word about the need for food. Carla, in turn, had called the church for help as well.

During the conversation, Bert had filled her in on all the details of the murder. Carla had helped Bert figure out a few things on other investigations and wanted her opinion. Much to Detective Mannor's dismay, they were a regular pair of amateur sleuths.

"What about the camera?"

"Don't you think it's a little strange?"

Bert shrugged. "I've seen homeless folks with stranger things. I mean, there once was a man I knew who owned a brand-new pickup truck, but was completely homeless. He slept in the bed of the truck during the summers and in the cab during the winter.

"No. What about that other story?" Carla thought out loud.

"What other story?" Bert asked, removing the plastic from the turkey and plopping it into a large baking tin.

"You know, the one in the paper about the camera shop being robbed multiple times this last month."

Sliding the turkey into the one vacant oven and turning up the heat, she turned around to face her friend. The thoughts bounced around her head as she began to realize what her friend was getting at. "Wait a second. You're saying that maybe our victim is also the culprit of the camera thefts?"

Carla snapped her fingers. "Bingo."

"Sometimes, you are brilliant, my friend."

Carla beamed. "I try."

"It's an interesting theory, that's for sure."

"Hey, maybe the camera shop owner is the murderer?"

Bert squinted in confusion, heading over to continue mixing the cinnamon, molasses, and brown sugar for the pecan pie. "How would that be possible?"

"I don't know. The owner tracks down whoever stole the equipment, tries to take it back, but ends up killing the guy."

"But why not just call in the police? I mean, they could easily have the culprit arrested and the merchandise returned."

Carla paused her chopping duties and looked over at Bert. "Oh, I guess you're right."

"I'm not saying it couldn't happen. Just seems unlikely."

"So much for me being brilliant," Carla groaned.

Bert knew her friend liked to speculate theories, but she often took them to extremes.

"No, it's still a good idea to consider. I've thought up crazier things that turned out to be correct." She quickly thought back to an earlier murder case she'd helped solve. Some of her ideas seemed off the wall bonkers at first, but had turned out to be right. How could she discount her own best friend's theories?

"It's possible, then?"

"In investigative work, you have to consider every possibility," Bert pointed out. Her mind was already racing with the clues. She thought of her schedule the following day and wondered if she would have time to swing by the camera shop in question to do a little investigating.

"It's kinda funny, huh?" Carla mused, returning to her chopping.

"What is?"

"How you keep getting mixed up in these murder cases, but then solve them."

Bert thought on it a moment and nodded. "I guess I just have a knack for this kind of stuff. I always had an eye for detail."

"You sure have."

"Anyway, I guess I'm just worried that the detective is going to end up pointing his finger at the wrong person, you know?"

"What, like you?" Carla laughed.

"No, I'm not so much worried about me." Bert glanced over at Shiv who was busy setting out plastic silverware and paper plates on a long serving table. She was exactly the kind of scapegoat the police might try to finger.

Who knew? Shiv had made a joke about robbing earlier. Based on her past, it was possible she had a few other items on her record.

The police ate that kind of thing up, and Shiv had been outside last before the body was found. Additionally, the detective's demeanor toward the girl had changed when he learned of her encounter with the victim.

Bert didn't know her that well, but she still felt an intrinsic kinship with the girl. No, she refused to let the detective pin it on her.

Shaking her head, she pushed any thoughts of the case out of her mind. "Anyway, no more talk about murder for now. We've got a meal to prepare."

CHAPTER 9

Just as darkness began to fall, Bert opened her doors to the hungry people who were waiting outside in the cold weather. Tiny dots of snowflakes fell, dancing in the streetlights and melting on the pavement.

It was the first snowfall of the season, but it didn't look like it was going to stay around.

Meanwhile, while things were growing cold and wet outside, the inside of Pies and Pages was full of warmth and holiday cheer. Volunteers helped guide the line in and through. Shiv, Andie, Bert, and Carla all stood behind the pie counter, serving up steaming slices of turkey, buttery piles of mashed potatoes, fluffy stuffing, and slices of cinnamon-sweet pecan pie.

It was amazing to watch how people's faces brightened up the further they got in the line. It was almost as if the shop had a warming effect that turned on the dimmer switch inside people. Bert's personal favorite was when families came through. It was sad that they were going without normal everyday comforts, especially the children, but Bert was simply thrilled to give them something to brighten their holiday.

It was a blessing that they had been able to relocate the dinner to the shop, otherwise none of these people would have a warm meal to eat.

Bert used her MP3 player and hooked it up to the speaker dock to play uplifting classical music to set the mood for the evening. All around, folks with happy smiles sat at the tables and chatted while they ate the food. It didn't seem to matter that a lot of it came out of a box or a can to these people. They were simply grateful.

"I'm going to take a quick break," Bert announced to her fellow workers as she slipped out of her apron. She walked over and picked up the carafe of coffee they had behind the counter. "I'm just going to see if anyone wants some more coffee in their cups."

"Good idea," Andie acknowledged.

Bert wanted to get out among the people, to see them enjoying their meals close up, and to hear their conversations. Being around people was invigorating, especially on happy occasions like Thanksgiving.

Passing through the tables, she offered her wares, filling mugs and making light conversation. The room was crowded, much smaller than the soup kitchen, but it seemed to be working well enough for the moment. A few people were sitting on the floor between bookshelves and eating their plates of food.

It was as she was walking along one of the aisles that a conversation caught her attention. Three people sat directly on the opposite side of the shelf, chatting.

"Did you guys hear why the soup kitchen was closed tonight? Another one dead, stabbed to death this time," a gruff sounding man said.

"I swear. It isn't safe for us out there on the streets anymore," a woman complained in return.

"Who was it this time?" A different man with a higher voice asked.

"Couldn't rightly tell ya'. I don't know the fella's name."

"He was new to the area?" the woman pressed.

"You could say that. I walked by that crime scene this morning and got a look at his face before they covered him up with a sheet. I've seen him a few times."

"And you didn't get his name?"

"Don't know. He never gave it, ya' understand."

"Ah, one of those quiet types," the woman assumed.

"No, not at all. The few times I met up with him in an alley or such, he wouldn't shut up. Was always askin' questions."

At this comment, Bert couldn't help but perk up a little more and listen.

"What kind of questions?"

"Oh, you know, about where we got food, water. Places we visited. He was a nosy chap, that's for sure."

"Did he seem off his rocker?" the woman asked, a hint of concern in her voice.

"Naw, he seemed fine in that respect. More of a pestering kinda fellow than anything else."

"Gives me the creeps," the woman said with a shiver in her voice.

"Makes you wonder who's going to die next."

"I don't want to talk about this anymore. Let's just enjoy the food," the woman insisted.

Bert quickly moved on, thinking about what she had just heard.

Makes you wonder who's going next. Those words stuck in her mind.

Well, if she had anything to say about it, no one else was going to get murdered—and she had a good idea where she could start her own little private investigation.

CHAPTER 10

I t was as the sun rose the next morning that Bert headed for the phone book. She'd spent the night in the cluttered upstairs apartment above the shop. She hadn't wanted to trouble any of her friends for a ride back to her cottage house on the other side of town. It was simply easier to stay at the shop.

She had to admit, despite the clutter and dust, she liked being able to pop up in the morning and just head down the stairs to work. She'd considered putting her house up for rent when she'd first bought the book shop. Now, however, she was certain she was ready for a change. She could downsize to the quaint apartment if it meant a shorter commute and being closer to Carla.

After showering and changing into some new clothes, ones she had brought to the shop a few weeks back in case of an emergency, she headed down and pulled out the phone book from under the counter. Running her finger down the pages, she found what she was looking for—the phone number for the Culver's Hood Newspaper.

Sliding her cell phone out of her pocket, she quickly dialed the number and waited.

After wading through a few automated menus, she was finally put through to a real person. "The Culver's Hood Newspaper. This is Tyla. How can I help you?"

"Hi, my name is Bertha Hannah, the owner of the Pies and Pages book shop."

"Oh, yes," the woman exclaimed excitedly. "We've just finished uploading the files."

"The . . . files?"

"Of course. One of our reporters caught wind of the dinner you hosted last night and wrote up a story on it."

Bert blinked, surprised by this news. "Oh, I didn't see any reporters here last night."

"Don't you worry. We like to be as discreet as possible. In many cases, we feel that we can better catch the true essence of a story when no one thinks they're being watched."

How come that didn't make Bert feel comfortable?

"However, if you're wanting to give an interview, I'm sure Tanner would love it."

"Tanner?"

"Yes, he's the reporter who wrote the story."

"Well, that's very flattering. However, I wasn't calling about that story." While having her pie and book shop in the newspaper the following day would be great advertisement and promotion, Bert hadn't called them up to learn about any story. She was more concerned about murder.

"Oh? You weren't aware of the story?"

"I had no idea about it."

"I see. In that case, how can I help you?"

"This reporter. Tanner. Is he the one who did the write up about the homeless murders?"

There was a long quiet pause, and Bert wondered if the call had been disconnected.

"How about I see if he's here in the office?" she finally suggested. There was a clicking noise followed by some elevator music. Bert tapped her fingers on the counter while she waited.

Only about a minute later, the line picked up again. "This is Tanner Wakeman. How can I help you?"

"Hi, Tanner. My name is Bert Hannah."

"Ah, yes. The woman who owns the Pies and Pages shop where the homeless Thanksgiving Dinner was held last night."

"Yes, that's right."

"I have to say, Mrs. Hannah, I was very impressed with your event."

"Well, it wasn't really my event. The real credit goes toward my friend Andie Right. She's the director of the soup kitchen here in Culver's Hood."

"Very good, very good." The sound of a pen scribbling on paper echoed over the line. Clearly, he assumed this was an interview.

"But, Mr. Tanner, I didn't call to discuss the dinner."

"Yes, our secretary mentioned your interest in another story."

"The homeless murders. Are you the man who wrote that story?"

There was a brief pause. "Yes, as a matter of fact, I am."

Bert hesitated on the next question. "Did you go undercover, I mean dress up as a bum, to look into that story?"

There was a confused hesitation. "No, I didn't."

"Did you do that last night?"

Another pause. "No, ma'am. None of our reporters were actually at the event. However, we had some photos delivered to us by those who were there."

Why did she get the feeling he was lying to her? What was he trying to cover up? Did he simply want to keep his reporting habits a secret?

Bert decided it wasn't worth pursuing and instead moved onto the next question. "Have any of your reporters gone missing lately?" she pressed.

"Excuse me?"

"Your reporters? Have any of them gone missing?"

"No, not that I'm aware of."

"Was anyone else working with you on the murder story?"

"No," he said flatly again. "Ma'am, do you mind me asking what this is all about?"

Did she dare share her hunch with a reporter? Deciding it was a bad idea, she skirted the question. "According to the police, no one was supposed to know that these deaths were actually murder. If you don't mind my asking, how did you come to learn about the poisonings?"

"I won't lie to you, I'm not supposed to share my sources. Confidentiality and all that."

"But, I'm not a reporter or the police. Can't you tell me?" she asked in a sweet tone.

He paused again. "Even if I knew, I couldn't. It was an anonymous tip that led me to that information."

"I see."

So much for her theory about the stabbing victim being an undercover reporter. With the conversation between the people at the dinner last night—talking about how much the man asked questions—she was sure it had to be an undercover reporter who had bit the dust.

Maybe Carla had been right in the first place. Maybe it really was the camera shop owner who had committed the stabbing. The rest of the deaths could be completely unrelated.

"Mrs. Hannah, do you know something about all of this?" Tanner cut into the silence.

"No. Not at all. I had a hunch, and it turns out I was wrong."

"You're not friends with the mayor, are you?"

Bert paused, raising one eyebrow. "No, why?"

"It's nothing."

However, by this comment alone, Bert knew exactly what he was getting at. It was apparent that he believed the mayor was somehow connected with these murders. It explained why he was being so secretive and hush-hush about the whole thing.

As unlikely as that possibility seemed, Bert wouldn't be surprised.

"Well, thank you for your help, anyway," she said, wanting to end the conversation.

"Mrs. Hannah," Tanner replied, stopping her before she could hang up.

"Yes?"

"What is your investment in this case?"

"A purely personal one. One of my oldest and dearest friends manages the soup kitchen."

"Andie Right?"

"Correct. Now, if you'll excuse me."

"Mrs. Hannah."

Repressing a groan, she rolled her eyes. "What?"

"I'm just going to warn you. Be careful. You don't know what kind of people you may be dealing with."

Bert opened her mouth to ask for clarification, but the line went completely silent.

CHAPTER 11

It was around eleven as Bert walked along the cold, windy streets of downtown Culver's Hood. The snow had begun to stick to the ground sometime during the morning, and a thin, almost superficial layer coated most of everything in patches of white.

Her mind was spinning around inside her head as she made her way toward her destination.

What had that reporter meant when he said to be careful? Who were these people she was supposedly dealing with? What did he know that he wasn't telling her?

The larger part of Bert's feelings told her that, logically, everything he'd said was hearsay. Did he really believe there was a conspiracy involving the mayor to get rid of the homeless? What for? Just to scare them off the streets of the city?

It seemed just a tad too much like a thriller novel for Bert to believe any of it.

No, she was still set on the fact that this was a singular person who had some sort of grudge—nothing else.

Which was what had convinced her to walk the seven blocks from Old Market to downtown in the snow. Pulling her scarf tight around her neck and adjusting her knit cap upon her head, she stopped at the corner of Eighth and Harmon. Glancing up, she read the swinging metal sign above the shop. The Corner Camera Store.

Entering the building, she let out a sigh of relief upon the instant greeting of the warmth. She was somewhat surprised to see so many customers milling about, but then remembered it was Black Friday. People were already starting their Christmas shopping.

An upbeat and poppy version of Jingle Bells, which Bert didn't care for, was echoing over the speakers.

"Welcome to The Corner Camera Store. How may I help you today?" came the exuberant greeting from the balding man behind the counter.

"Hi," Bert replied, putting on the best smile possible. Walking up to the counter, she placed her gloved hands on the glass case a looked in at the merchandise. "Are you the owner?"

"Yes, I am. Looking for anything in particular?"

"Yes, actually. I saw this tiny little camera on someone the other day, a young man. It was a square about the size of a brownie."

The man held up a finger. "Ah, you must mean the GoAdventure. It's a durable little thing, very small, and easy to wear. It can take discreet shots while doing any activity."

"I think that's the one," she said, continuing the conversation.

"I'm a little low on stock at the moment, but I could order you one for next week."

"You're low on stock?" she asked, feigning surprise. Then she made a face of recognition, purposefully widening her eyes. "Oh, are you the shop that was robbed? The one I read about in the paper."

At this comment, his face twanged with a hint of anger. "Why, yes. It is unfortunate, but they stole a few of our GoAdventures. We only ended up having one left."

"Oh, so you still have one in stock?"

He shook his head. "No, sorry. I didn't mean to imply that I had any left. You see, one of my regulars from the local college bought the last one a few days ago."

"A student?"

"We do get a lot of students here from the communications and art departments, but this was one of the department heads. He told me he's working on a project of his own."

She nodded. "Ah, I see."

"However, like I said, I can put one on order for you, Mrs.?"

"Hannah."

"Would you like me to order one, Mrs. Hannah? I could have it in as soon as next week."

Bert glanced back over her shoulder as the bell over the door dinged. A young blonde-haired man smiled and waved at the cashier.

"Is that him, the guy who bought the GoAdventure?" Bert pressed.

"Oh, no. He's a student from the college. He always buys his film from me."

The man came over and stood at the counter. His scruffy, unshaven beard couldn't hide his baby face. "Hi, Rich."

"Looking for some more film, Skylar?"

"You know it."

"I think I'll just browse a bit, thank you," Bert chimed in, letting them get to their business. Heading down one of the aisles, she kept her eyes on the men as they talked. Just as she had assumed, the shop keeper hardly seemed like the kind of man who could kill someone.

It didn't mean it wasn't possible, it just seemed more and more unlikely.

"So, any more merchandise go missing?" the young man named Skylar asked while the shop keepers grabbed a few boxes of film.

Bert was surprised that people were still using actual film, but assumed that it was for a specific project. Maybe he was trying to capture images in a certain style that only film could provide. She didn't know much on the topic but knew how creative some of the local college students could be.

"No, thankfully."

"And the cops never caught the guy?" he asked digging into his pocket for his wallet.

"No, not yet. Whoever, it is did it right under my nose, while I was in the shop, and I never even noticed." He set the items on the counter.

Handing the money over, exact change in ones and quarters by the looks of it, he paid for the film. "I'm telling you, man. You need to get a better security system. Surveillance cameras, alarm tags on the high price items."

The shop keeper put up both hands. "I know, I know. You're right Skylar. You'll be happy to hear that I have contacted a company and they're sending someone at the end of the day today to give me an estimate."

Skylar smirked wryly. "I'm glad to hear it. Well, thanks for the film."

"Yeah. Maybe next time you come in, I'll be all decked out."

"I'm looking forward to it. See ya, man," he waved.

"Bye," he nodded, moving his concentration to the next customer in line who had her arms full of a whole array of items.

Bert kept her eyes on the young college student, not quite sure why his attitude had been so off-putting. Was it simply his attitude or something more?

He squeezed in between shoppers, moving for the exit.

That was when she saw it.

Skylar's hand passed over a nearby stand of HDMI cables and headphones. In one swoop, he had one of each in his hands and had slipped them into his large wool jacket.

Bert's jaw dropped wide open as he nonchalantly walked out of the shop. She'd just seen him shoplift. Did that mean he was the same person who had hit the shop before, stealing the GoAdventures?

Bert didn't wait around. She pushed past all the eager Christmas shoppers and out into the freezing cold day.

Looking both up and down the street, she realized the young man had disappeared.

She'd lost him.

CAROLYN Q. HUNTER

CHAPTER 12

Bert hadn't expected to find herself sitting in the passenger seat of Detective Mannor's black, undercover, cop car that day, yet here she was right next to him as they made their way toward the college campus.

After she'd lost track of Skylar, she knew she couldn't just wait around. She'd seen a crime and needed to report it.

Much to her surprise, Detective Mannor was the one to show up on the scene—further confirming her assumptions that there was at least some sort of small connection between the camera shop, the thefts, and the stabbing.

What those connections were, she was at a loss. If anything, all of these clues made the investigation more confusing.

"I hope you know you're only here because I need you to identify the thief," he pointed out. "You're my only witness to this crime."

Bert folded her arms and leaned back in the chair, glad he hadn't decided to have her ride in the back behind the cage just out of spite. "I'm aware, detective, but why exactly did they send the homicide division to look into this?"

"I can't comment on an ongoing investigation. I'm sure you, of all people, know that better than most."

"It's true, I don't think I could hear those words in anyone else's tone of voice but yours," she joked with a biting sarcasm.

Mannor grunted unhappily in return. "Maybe if you kept your nose out of police business, like I've warned you on multiple occasions, you wouldn't have to hear me say it."

"Look, would you rather I hadn't reported this theft? Huh? I could have just acted like so many other people and said, 'It's none of my business'."

"No, of course you should report a crime when you see it. However, after you've made you report and given me a statement, your job is done."

"Clearly, that isn't the case, since you're taking me along to the college."

He tapped the steering wheel with a flat hand. "You're an eyewitness. It's your job to help identify the suspect so I can make the proper steps to bring him in." Pulling up into the campus' administration lot, he took the liberty of parking in the official campus security designated spot. Putting the car into park, he turned off the engine. "Now, from here on out, no more questions. Just do as you're told, and we won't have any more problems."

"Fine by me," she sighed, wishing she didn't have to spend part of her day with the irritable man. She knew he had saved her life on one occasion, but she wasn't sure that gave him the right to treat her so harshly.

She knew she had a way of pushing his buttons, and he certainly pushed hers, but did that mean he had to constantly treat her like such a nuisance?

"Follow me, don't say anything unless I tell you to," he ordered, stepping out into the snow.

Groaning inwardly, Bert followed suit, straining to figure out how to smooth things over with the detective. She hoped she could keep from opening her mouth and fighting back against him. Unfortunately, that was just her nature.

Walking into the building's lobby, the detective seemed to intrinsically know his way to the Records and Registration office.

"Good afternoon. How may I . . ." The young woman behind the desk let her voice trail off as she saw the detective holding out his badge.

"My name's Detective Mannor. I need to talk to your supervisor."

"R-Right away officer," she stuttered, heading off to the back room. A few moments later, a man with a large belly and wearing a tweed jacket walked out of the room. The big bushy mustache couldn't hide his genial smile.

"Detective Mannor. Good to see you. What can I do for you this fine day?"

"Carl, we're looking for a young man who attends this college, first name Skylar."

The man clasped his hands in front of himself. "Is he in some sort of trouble, detective?"

"He may be a key witness in a homicide case," Mannor replied without mentioning the theft at the camera shop.

"I see. Why don't you step into my office and we can have a look?"

Detective Mannor bowed slightly in thanks and followed the man behind the counter. Bert stayed close behind.

"Oh, is she with you?" the supervisor asked, eyeballing Bert with one eyebrow raised in suspicion. The expression made him appear like a villain from an old silent movie.

"She's an eye witness who can identify the boy we're looking for."

"Very well," he agreed, opening the door and allowing them entry into his cramped office space. It was cluttered with various files, folders, papers, and food wrappers. The walls were lined with photographs of all of the different department heads. Many of them weren't straight and it bothered Bert to no end.

How such an unorganized and cluttered man could keep a job at a well-respected college was beyond her.

"Go ahead, have a seat."

The detective and Bert both slid into the uncomfortable wooden chairs.

"Now, what did you say this young man's name was?"

"Uh, Skylar," Bert announced.

"First name?" he pressed.

"That's correct," the detective confirmed.

"And last name?"

Bert glanced over at Mannor, but he offered her no help. "I don't know the last name."

That eyebrow shot up dramatically again, making the supervisor look silly. "You don't have his full name? How in the dickens do you expect me to be able to help you that way?"

"All I got was a first name," she admitted.

"Well, there could be fifty Skylar's alone at this school."

Mannor leaned forward on the desk, an old chocolate wrapper crinkling under one elbow. "Do you have pictures on file?"

"Well, of course we do. That's how we make the student IDs."

"Then, we'll just have to look through all those images, if you don't mind pulling them up." He put on his best smile, which wasn't very convincing. He'd done a better job looking happy with Shiv— probably because he liked her more.

Giving a groan of complaint, the man agreed and typed in the search into the system. "There, you see. Just over twenty names," he turned the computer screen toward them, showing a list of images and names.

"It isn't fifty, is it?" Detective Mannor retorted.

Bert nearly laughed out loud upon hearing this comment, hardly able to believe her ears. Had the detective just made a biting joke? She guessed that even he had a tiny sense of humor.

"Go ahead, Mrs. Hannah. See if you recognize any of the photos."

Nodding, she began the process of slowly examining each face to see if anyone matched the young man she'd seen at the camera store. It was only about five in when she spotted him. "There," she said with a point of her finger.

Mannor leaned in and read the name. "Skylar Roundhouse. Communications department."

Bert instinctively started looking at the images on the wall for the head of the communications department. She assumed he would want to know about the student's criminal behavior.

"So, there he is," the supervisor mumbled.

"Now, was that so hard?" the detective pointed out. "Now, do you mind calling up his address for me?"

"I'd usually require a warrant for this kind of information," he complained, but not stopping the process of pulling up the information.

Finally, Bert's eyes rested on the communication director and she gasped loudly. "Detective," she exclaimed.

"Just a minute, Mrs. Hannah," he instructed, pulling out his notepad as he watched the screen.

"Detective, you need to look at this."

"Let me copy this information," he told her.

"Detective," she insisted, pulling on his sleeve.

"What, Mrs. Hannah?" he snapped, frustrated at being interrupted.

"That man in the picture, the head of the communication department. Does he look familiar?" she pointed up at the portrait on the wall.

Mannor's eyes followed the path of her finger, his gaze resting on the man's face. Instantly, he recognized him. "Is that?"

"Our murder victim," Bert confirmed.

CHAPTER 13

"W"here is the communications director?" Mannor demanded, putting his hands on his desk and looking the mousy man in the face.

"I thought you were looking for this Skyler?"

"This is important. Where is the communications director?"

"Well, like most of the staff, he's probably off celebrating his Thanksgiving. There is only a handful of us left on campus this weekend, mostly doing catchup work."

"Are you positive he's out with family?"

"I have no idea. I can look up the notes on his file, if you want."

"Please," the detective insisted with a strained smile of politeness.

After a few more taps of the keys and a click of the mouse, he had the file pulled up. "It looks like he's on sabbatical this semester to work on a research project."

"What project?" Mannor insisted.

"I don't know. His specialty is journalism, so maybe he's trying to compile some info on a story—probably something big."

"Wait a minute, did you say journalism?" Bert pressed, jumping into the conversation.

"Yeah, so what?"

Bert glanced up at Mannor. "I think I have an idea of what's going on, Detective."

"And?" he asked.

"I'd have to confirm my theory first. Maybe he kept some sort of notes, took some pictures, anything to point us in the right direction."

"Can't you just tell me?" he asked.

"If I'm wrong. . ." she let her voice trail off.

Mannor, without even a second thought, turned to the man behind the desk. "I need access to the communication director's office."

* * *

Ten minutes later, they were in the communication department's main office, facing the director's doorway as Carl slipped the master key in and unlatched the lock.

"Now, don't touch a darn thing. I'll do the looking," he ordered Bert while shaking his index finger at her.

"Not a problem," she agreed. They were finally hot on the right trail, it seemed. If it meant finally catching this murderer once and for all, she'd try to follow the detective's instructions to a T.

As the door swung open, the detective charged in.

"I usually would need a search warrant for this too," the chubby man muttered under his breath, but Bert heard him.

"Then why let the detective in, if you're so worried about it?"

He put up both hands defensively. "I'm not. I just don't want a big hassle over all this."

Bert rolled her eyes and walked in behind Mannor. Every wall of the office was lined with shelves of books, folders, and photography equipment. The desk itself had a name plaque, along with papers, pens, and files.

"Don't touch anything," he reminded her.

"You already said that," she returned with her own snappy remark.

He was already opening the filing cabinet and flipping through files for anything that might stick out. "And yet, somehow, you don't always seem to listen to me when I tell you to do something."

She scanned over the room for anything strange or unique that stood out to her. An image, even a word or phrase, might lead them in the right direction.

The detective moved over to the desk, sat in the chair, and began opening the drawers and rifling through them.

At that same moment, a manila folder on the corner of the desk caught Bert's eye. It was labeled with one singular word: Poison. Without another thought, she picked it up and opened it. The news clippings, images, and notes led her to the correct conclusion. "Hey, I think this is it. This is what we are looking for."

"I told you not to touch anything."

"Just as I thought. He went undercover as a homeless man to look into these poisonings."

"What? Give me that," he blurted out.

She went on reading without giving it to him. "And . . ." she paused, her breath catching in her chest.

"What? What did he find?"

"He tracked the deaths, the poisonings, back to the soup kitchen." She hated the implications of what this could mean. Andie had strict rules about non-volunteers not coming behind the counter into the kitchen. The only volunteer who was consistent enough to continually poison the soup was Shiv. "She has to be bringing the poison in, in her pockets, her purse, something like that, since the kitchen doesn't have any of its own," she whispered.

The detective snatched the paperwork from her hands and scanned over it. "Come on. We're going down to that kitchen right this instant."

CHAPTER 14

"Stay in the car," Detective Mannor ordered Bert as they pulled onto the street just outside the alleyway. The police tape was still in place and Bert's car was still sitting where it had been left the day before.

"Now, wait a minute."

"Don't argue with me. It was bad enough that you came into the victim's office, and that you were touching things." He popped open his door.

"Hey, you didn't stop me," she retorted, knowing it was a useless dispute.

"And now I am. Stay here."

"But, I'm the one who figured this all out."

"And I'm the professional police detective, so stay put," he demanded, sliding out and making his way under the tape. A moment later, he disappeared inside the back door.

Sighing, Bert slumped down in the passenger seat while she waited. What did he expect to find in there? Rat poison? If so, he was going to be sorely disappointed. Andie had specifically said she never kept any rat poison on the premises.

If Shiv was adding the poison to the soup or other foods in the kitchen, she was sneaking it in.

The one thing that was still majorly bothering Bert was why? Why would a young woman like that, someone who had relied on charitable services such as the soup kitchen, also try and kill others in the same situation?

Did she have some sort of hidden grudge under the surface, hiding behind the gentle and pretty exterior?

Shaking her head, Bert opened her door to let the chilly late autumn air into the car. She breathed deeply, drinking in the crisp freshness of the day, something that seemed to help ease her stress around this whole chaotic situation.

Swinging her feet out of the car, she stood up and let out a heavy breath and it turned to steam in the air in front of her.

A light honk on a car horn caused her to jump, ripping her from her deep thoughts. Spinning toward the back end of the police car, she was surprised to see Andie parked there, smiling and waving.

Letting out a sigh of relief, Bert walked over as the passenger window was rolled down.

"Hey, Bert, what are you doing standing out here?" Andie asked.

"I got stuck tagging along while the detective went in to do some more snooping around. We think we've almost got this case solved."

"Well, thank heaven for that. I would prefer to have my soup kitchen in good working order before the rush of the Christmas season hits us full swing. I was just dropping by to see if they were done with things."

"And I'd like to have my car back," Bert agreed with a slight laugh.

"Speaking of, do you need a ride back to your shop? Does the detective need you to stick around?"

"I doubt it," she noted, opening the passenger door and sliding in.

For a moment, Bert considered whether or not she should tell the detective that she was leaving. Finally, she decided that he would likely be happier to find out that she was gone. "I'm sure he'll be thrilled that I'm not sitting around in his car."

"Shall we, then?" Andie laughed.

"We shall."

Putting the car back into drive, Andie pulled out onto the street and continued along the snowy pavement toward Old Market. "So, what is it that you and the detective discovered? You said he was getting close to an answer?"

"Only because I helped him," she pointed out.

"If I'm not mistaken, Bert, you've helped out a couple times now."

"Detective Mannor hardly seems happy about it, trust me. If I was smart, I'd just keep my nose out of it."

Andie glanced over at her friend. "Why don't you? I mean, what is your personal investment in the cases?"

"Hey, when you find some poor person's dead body, you just feel some sort of obligation to them." She gave a little shrug. Opening her purse, she began to rifle through for her lip balm. The sudden onset of the cold weather had dried out her skin considerably. "If it wasn't my personal friends who were always the ones involved, like you, I wouldn't even bother. I'd butt out just like the detective wants."

Andie whistled a quiet laugh. "You never were one to let someone in need go by, especially if you suspected some sort of injustice."

"I guess, that's so," she agreed, digging all the way to the bottom of her purse. She really didn't care for purses. She liked things to be neat and orderly, but most purse designs made that impossible. Even if she always tried to keep her lip balm on the right inside pocket, it seemed to just fall out and get mixed in with everything else.

"Missing something?"

"My lip balm. This snow is really drying me out."

"I get it."

"Do you have any?" Bert asked, instinctively popping open the glove box to check inside.

"Wait, don't open that," Andie shouted.

It was too late. Bert paused with her heart hammering in her chest as she stared at the odd and unexpected contents inside.

Laying among some scattered papers and receipts was a box of rat poison along with a bloody kitchen knife.

CHAPTER 15

Bert's voice was hesitant, like dry cotton was caught in her throat, before she could manage to whisper her question. "Andie? What is all this?"

"I-It isn't what it looks like," her friend argued, reaching over and slamming the glove box shut.

"Then what is it, Andie? Because it looks like you've got a bloody knife in your car—maybe the knife used to stab that poor man in the alleyway."

Turning the car down the road at the next intersection, Andie sped up her pace along the icy pavement. "Look, I found the knife in Shiv's purse, so I took it and hid it here in my car."

"But why? Why not just hand it off to the police?" Bert noticed they were no longer heading the direction of the Old Market district.

"Shiv is a great volunteer. She's like a daughter to me. Even if she killed the guy, I couldn't let her take the fall for it."

Bert put her hands on the dashboard. "But she's a murderer, Andie, and you've implicated yourself in the crime as well."

"Not if you don't tell that detective of yours," Andie whispered, a hint of threat in her voice.

"How can I do that? How can I withhold evidence from a very serious police investigation? Don't you realize this is a crime?" Glancing at a sign, Bert saw that they were headed toward the riverfront.

"I know that, Bert. Don't you think I'd know that?"

"What about the poison?"

Sighing, Andie shook her head. "I took that off Shiv last week, too. It was in her purse."

Bert didn't say it, but found it a little odd that her friend was constantly poking through the volunteer's purse.

"I realized she'd been the one who was poisoning the poor homeless people, killing them. I figured she was probably sprinkling it in their soup bowls. Little by little, she was giving it to them until they got sick and died."

Bert couldn't believe her ears. Shaking her head, she slapped the dashboard. "Dang it, Andie. If Shiv really is doing all this, you can't keep protecting her. She's not right in the head. She needs help."

"You don't understand anything," Andie hissed, her brow wrinkling and her cheeks flushing angrily.

Bert's heart beat a little faster as she had a sickening realization, something she didn't want to believe. "You know, the poisonings weren't public knowledge until just a few days ago, on Wednesday to be exact." Leaning over, she tried to look into her friend's eyes. "How, by finding the poison in Shiv's purse, were you able to deduce that?"

Her mouth hung open, searching for the right words. "I-I meant, that I saw her putting it in the soup."

"No, you said you figured she must have been doing it, not that you'd seen it."

"Well, I misspoke, then."

Bert glanced at the glove box out of the corner of her eye, wondering if she'd be able to get a hold of the knife quick enough if she needed to. "Are you sure about that?"

"What are you trying to imply, Bert?" she snapped, pulling into the parking lot along the side of Missouri River. A walkway ran along the rushing water.

Bert was sure it was freezing.

"You know exactly what I'm saying," she shot back.

"Why accuse me? What possible reason could I have for murdering the homeless, the very people I've spent most of my life trying to help?"

"I have no idea. Why don't you tell me?"

"You're wrong," she shouted.

"Am I? You're one of my oldest friends, but that doesn't mean I'll cover up for you."

"Some friend you are," she spat.

"So, it's true then?"

"No, it's not."

Bert discreetly scooted forward in her seat, trying to be closer to the glove box. "I can tell you why you stabbed that gentleman in the alley. He wasn't homeless at all. He was a college professor, specializing in journalism, and he was investigating the poisonings. He probably tipped off the newspaper to the story. Then, he figured out where the source of the poisonings was. He even had a micro camera—a GoAdventure—that he was using to take pictures. That's why he was so adamant to get into the kitchen."

"You're insane."

"Am I? I think you realized he was getting close to figuring out your scheme, and you took matters into your own hands and stabbed him to death. You also smashed the camera, but I bet the police can still pull off the pictures."

In a lightning second, Andie was leaping across the center console at her old friend, her hands grasping for her throat. "Darn you, darn you, darn you," she screamed.

Bert put up both hands to defend herself, shutting her eyes as the hands gripped at her throat.

A moment later, a burst of freezing cold air hit her in the face, and the venomous hands retreated. Opening her eyes, she saw Andie being dragged backward out the driver side door. "That's enough, Mrs. Right," Detective Mannor ordered, pulling her arms behind her back and handcuffing her.

"Are you okay, Bert?" he asked.

"I-I think so," she called back.

Andie struggled against the restraints with the look of a wild dog upon her face. "You don't understand. No one understands. If I thought I could truly offer them a better life, I would do that instead. But with the new attitude of the mayor, of the city council, of all the entitled people in this city, I've received less and less resources to help these people."

"The solution is to commit murder instead?" Bert found her voice cracked and shouting as she slid out of the passenger side door.

"Their lives don't mean much. They won't ever amount to anything in this society. The best they can hope for is the peace of death."

Bert couldn't believe her ears. "Everyone deserves a chance at life, as many chances as they can get. You don't have the right to make that choice."

Mannor shook his head. "Come along, Mrs. Right. I think it's best we go down to the station."

CHAPTER 16

"The safe in her office was stuffed full of boxes of rat poison," Detective Mannor informed Bert, taking a seat at the table across from her.

The pie shop owner sat with her head low, her hands cradling a mug of coffee. The low hum of Christmas music rang over the radio in the corner. An array of notes and recipe cards, ideas for a new holiday-themed pie for the upcoming month of December. It was all doing so little to cheer her up.

"So, that's how you knew it was her?"

"I suspected, yes. I came back outside just as you two were pulling away from the soup kitchen, so I followed along."

"And Shiv? What about her?"

"I haven't found anything to implicate her in any of this."

Bert hummed quietly in thought. "Why didn't Shiv see the body when she showed up?"

"Mrs. Right had covered the body completely in trash bags, assuming no one would spot it until trash day the following week."

"But one of the bags fell down when I drove my car into the alley?"

"It seems likely. That's why you spotted him."

"So, my old friend is a murderer and even tried to pin it on an innocent girl."

Mannor sighed, sipping his own coffee. The scent of peppermint wafted from his Koffee Hous travel mug. He sure seemed to enjoy his seasonal drinks. "I know you've known her for a number of years. I realize how hard this might be."

Bert gave a little nod. "I just never would have suspected it, that's all."

"We found the micro SD card in her purse, and that basically clinched it."

"The micro SD?"

"Yes, the one that was taken from the GoAdventure before it was smashed. It contained enough evidence to put her away for a good long time."

"What was going through her head?" Bert wondered out loud.

"Nothing good. My guess is she'll plead insanity and be granted it."

Bert nodded. "You'd have to be a little crazy to slowly kill multiple people."

"The one good thing to come out of this is that the mayor is starting to change her tune about the homeless. I think she feels sorry for what's been happening. Either that, or she's putting on a good face. She and the city council are working hard to find a suitable replacement for Mrs. Right."

Bert gave a half smile. "I'm glad to hear it. So many people need the help."

"They've also set up an ambulance that'll go around and check people for rat poisoning for free. She's paying for that out of her own pocket."

"That's good."

"Anyway, I was only able to figure things out more quickly thanks to you."

Bert blinked, looking up at him with shocked eyes.

"Now, don't go getting any ideas. I'm not recruiting you for the force or anything, and you still stepped way outside your bounds . . . again."

"I know, and I'm sorry about that," she finally admitted.

"And I would have figured it out eventually with or without you."

Bert refrained from rolling her eyes.

"However, we were able to prevent any more murders by solving this faster."

"I should be the one thanking you. You saved my skin again."

Mannor stood up with an uncomfortable grunt. "Don't worry about it. That's my job."

"And what about Skylar, the college kid?"

"We had two of our uniforms pick him up at his dorm room. He had all the stolen merchandise hidden away in his desk drawers. I guess he got his kicks by swiping stuff on a regular basis."

"So, he had nothing to do with these murders."

"Not a thing."

Bert stood up as well. "Well, Detective, I appreciate you coming out to check up on me. I know you have better things to do."

Mannor shuffled his feet back and forth. "I knew she was a friend of yours, and I figured that would be hard."

"I'll be okay. It's officially the Christmas season, after all. The season of peace and miracles."

He nodded. "There is one other thing I wanted to talk to you about."

"What's that, Detective?"

Digging into his pocket, he brought out two pieces of paper—tickets by the looks of it. "Well, you see, the historic movie theater here in the Old Market often shows older movies on the big screen. This next month, in December, they're showing Santa Claus Versus the Martians." His voice was growing thinner, like it was drying out. "I know you said you enjoy old cheesy sci-fi movies, so I thought you might want to go."

Bert blinked her eyes at the detective, hardly able to believe her ears. "A-Are you asking me on a date, Detective?"

"I thought it would be fun to go together," he confirmed, not directly answering her question, but answering it none-the-less.

She couldn't think of anything to say in response. This man, this hardened police detective, the same one who'd snapped at her and put her in her place on multiple occasions, was asking her out on a date. Unfortunately, she just wasn't sure she was ready for anything like that.

Not yet.

"Detective, I appreciate the offer, but I think I'm going to have to pass." She gave him a shrug before sitting back down to work on her new recipe for that year's Christmas pie.

"I see. Well, if you change your mind, you have my cell phone number."

"Yes, I do."

"The tickets are for this Friday, December first."

"If I change my mind, Detective, I'll call you," she confirmed.

"Good. By the way, you can call me Harold."

"Goodbye, Detective," she said with a little nod.

He hesitated for a second, but then shuffled out the door, letting the bell ring as he left.

Once he was gone, Bert couldn't help but let a smile creep up on the corners of her lips. Wait until Carla heard about this one.

Made in the USA
Coppell, TX
03 November 2023

23768540R00095